ELEPHLOOPS AND WIZZAROOS

By Celeste Yost
Illustrations By Reese Barron

Copyright 2015 Celeste Yost. All rights reserved.

No part of this book may be reproduced, stored in a retrieval system, or transmitted by any means without the written permission of the author.

ISBN: - 13: 978-1508774310

ISBN: - 10: 1508774315

Printed in the United States of America

WITH LOVE TO THE CHERUBS, AARON, JACK AND REESE

PREFACE

I wrote the verse for this book in 2005 when my granddaughter, Reese, was born. Her brother, Jack, was two-and-a-half at the time and referred to elephants as "Elephloops. Our family thought that was so comical. I thought the subject of elephloops might make for some interesting reading.

Jack is twelve now and I recently came across the manuscript. As I was reading it, I thought it would be fun to ask Reese, now ten years old, if she might like to illustrate it. Being very creative and funny, she was thrilled to undertake the task of collaborating with Gram.

Reese has drawn all the illustrations in this book with only some slight modification by me.

Thank you, Jack and Reese, for your inspiration and talents. Grandchildren are, indeed, a joy!

Elephloops and wizzaroos went downtown to buy some shoes.

On the way they met a bear who said he'd like to buy a pair.

'Round the corner near a wall
stood an ostrich six feet tall.

"I need fancy shoes," she cried,
"There's a wedding! I'm the bride!"

Two turtles and a squirrel came too,
and a snake whose tongue was blue.

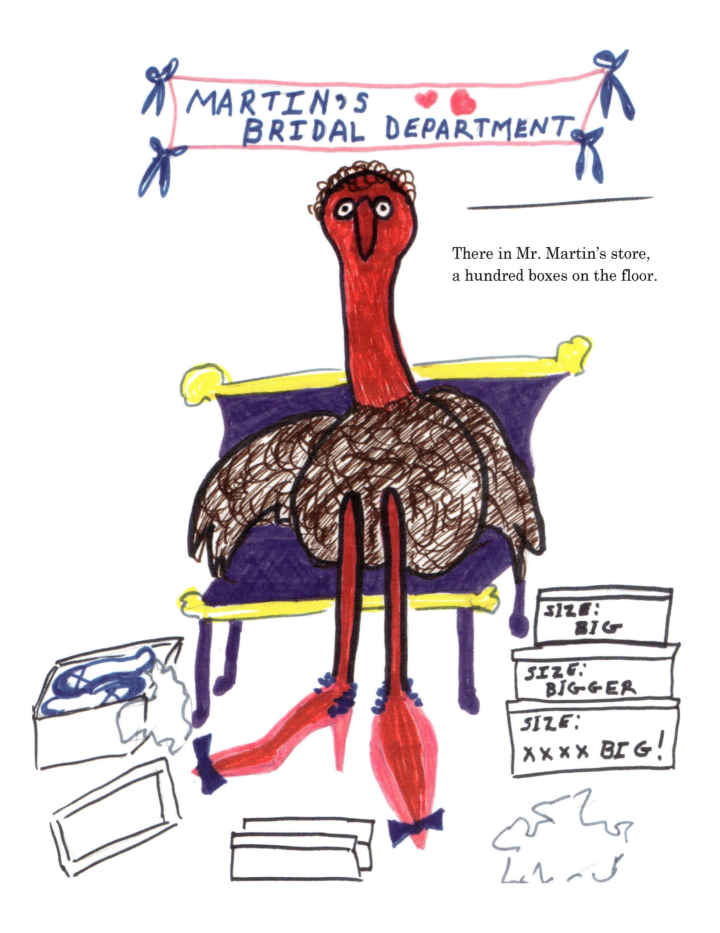

There in Mr. Martin's store,
a hundred boxes on the floor.

Shoes were here and shoes were there. Shoes and more shoes everywhere!

Some had laces, some had snaps, silly ruffles, furry flaps.

See the toeshoes on this wall?
The elephloop has tried them all.

"In these toeshoes," said the girl, "you could dance and turn and twirl!"

The elephloop said, "Yes, I could! I might even be quite good!"

She tied them up right to her knee,
and balanced most precariously.

The first twirl took her near the door.
The second put her on the floor!

She gladly took the toeshoes off,
"They're not for me! I've had enough!"

The wedding section was extensive. The ostrich said, "They're SO expensive!"

She tried on white, then pink, then blue.
She didn't know just what to do.

The heels were all too high and thin.
She couldn't fit her wide feet in.

It wasn't working out at all.
In high heels, she was just too tall.

In the corner near the back, running shoes were on a rack.

The turtles tried on running shoes.

With these," they said, "we'll never lose the race against that crazy hare.

"We'll run so fast and leave him there!"

"We each need four," one turtle said.
The other turtle shook his head.

"That's four too many shoes to tie.
I'm tired already, let's not try!"

They joined the others in the chair and sighing, waited for the bear.

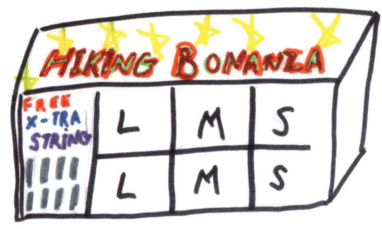

Hiking boots were just his thing
with straps and flaps and extra string.

"But they're not comfortable at all.
They're too short and I'm too tall."

All the animals were sad. Things were looking very bad.
Some shoes were just too short and tight, none at all that fit just right.

They thought about what they could do, but no one seemed to have a clue.
The snake just watched without a word. Shoes for him were just absurd.

And what about the Wizzaroos?
They don't even care for shoes.

They just came to watch the rest
choose the shoes that they like best.

The squirrel was silent all the while
then to her friends, said with a smile,

"We're animals, we don't need shoes.
Our feet are best for what we do."

They all agreed she used her head
they'd happily wear feet instead!

Made in the USA
Lexington, KY
21 March 2015